"A *friendly*! Against ~~~~~~~~~~~~ said Leroy at break. "What a joke! Most probably none of us will survive. In fact, that's probably what Mrs Kingsley's hoping for. Then she'll have a nice quiet school."

"But we've got Miss Brown," I said. "You heard her. She's never lost a match."

"She says!"

"Yeah," said Danny, "and I bet none of her other teams ever played Church Street . . ."

A fast and funny footballing story, ideal for building reading confidence.

www.booksattransworld.co.uk/childrens

YOUNG CORGI BOOKS

Young Corgi books are perfect when you are looking for great books to read on your own. They are full of exciting stories and entertaining pictures. There are funny books, scary books, spine-tingling stories and mysterious ones. The books are written by some of the most famous and popular of today's children's authors, and by some of the best new talents, too.

Whether you read one chapter a night, or devour the whole book in one sitting, you'll love Young Corgi books. The more you read, the more you'll want to read!

Other Young Corgi books to get your teeth into:
SAMMY'S SUPER SEASON by Lindsay Camp
THE GUARD DOG by Dick King-Smith
A WITCH IN THE CLASSROOM! by Ghillian Potts

Also available by Paul May:

Published by Corgi Pups, for beginner readers:

CAT PATROL!

Published by Corgi Yearling, for junior readers:

TROUBLEMAKERS
DEFENDERS

NICE ONE, SMITHY!

Paul May

Illustrated by Kate Sheppard

NICE ONE, SMITHY!
A YOUNG CORGI BOOK: 0 552 547204

PRINTING HISTORY
Young Corgi edition published 2002

1 3 5 7 9 10 8 6 4 2

Copyright © Paul May, 2002
Illustrations copyright © Kate Sheppard, 2002

The right of Paul May to be identified as the author of this work has been
asserted in accordance with the Copyright, Designs and Patents Act 1988

Set in 17/21pt Bembo Schoolbook by Falcon Oast Graphic Art Ltd

Young Corgi Books are published by Transworld Publishers,
61–63 Uxbridge Road, London W5 5SA,
a division of The Random House Group Ltd,
in Australia by Random House Australia (Pty) Ltd,
20 Alfred Street, Milsons Point, Sydney, NSW 2061, Australia,
in New Zealand by Random House New Zealand Ltd,
18 Poland Road, Glenfield, Auckland 10, New Zealand
and in South Africa by Random House (Pty) Ltd,
Endulini, 5a Jubilee Road, Parktown 2193, South Africa

Printed and bound in Great Britain by
Cox & Wyman Ltd, Reading, Berkshire

For Tom

Chapter One
Teachers

This is me. Fizz Parker. That's what
everyone calls me. Well, almost everyone. I can't help it that my mum
called me Felicity. She says it's a *pretty*
name – I ask you! It wouldn't be so
bad if it wasn't for the teachers. I even
went to Mrs Kingsley – she's our
headteacher – and I said to her,

"Please, Mrs Kingsley, why can't the teachers call me Fizz?"

"We don't use nicknames in class, Felicity," she said.

"But you told us people shouldn't call other people names they don't like," I said. "It's a school rule."

"That's different," Mrs Kingsley snapped. "Felicity is the name you were born with. You should be used to it by now."

How unreasonable can you get? I wouldn't have told *you*, of course, but you were bound to find out. Only it's not my fault, so don't laugh, right?

If you want to laugh, you can laugh at this lot. There's Smithy, Sanjay, Leroy, Danny and Jack. We're all in Class Five at Hillside Primary, and we're all crazy about football. Only, until this year our lives were a misery and a torment.

The trouble was our teachers. The only decent one was Mrs MacKay. She was the only one of them who didn't actually *hate* football, and she had to go and have a baby. When Mrs MacKay left, we had supply teachers. And you know what *they're* like.

Mrs Lamb was the first one. She didn't last long. Ronaldo, the guinea pig, escaped one lunch-time, and she found him eating her sandwiches. It wasn't Ronaldo's fault. He can't resist lettuce, and Mrs MacKay told us it's cruel to keep animals caged up all day and all night. So it's always been Smithy's special job to exercise Ronaldo at break times.

Mrs Lamb went very still when she saw him. I thought he looked sweet, nibbling away like that, but Mrs Lamb sent Smithy to fetch Mrs Kingsley. Mrs Lamb went *on* and *on* about how it was dirty and disgusting having a guinea pig running wild in the classroom – which isn't fair because Ronaldo is a very clean guinea pig, and not wild at all. The next day, Mr Muggs arrived.

You'd think a man would like football, wouldn't you? Not Mr Muggs. I heard him telling Mrs Kingsley that we were an unruly mob, and there were easier ways of earning a living. I thought that was very rude of him. Mrs MacKay used to tell us that we were full of natural bounce and enthusiasm.

And then there was Mrs Bird. Mrs Bird looked OK, but you just can't tell, can you?

Chapter Two

It Came Out of Nowhere

It happened at play-time, on a Friday
morning. I was in goal. Smithy was
streaking down the wing and I was
hopping up and down, getting ready
to make a brilliant save. Then Leroy's
little sister, Rosie, ran in front of
Smithy and grabbed the ball. She's
always doing that. It drives us crazy.

"Hey! Give that back!" Smithy yelled.

"Don't shout at Rosie," said Leroy angrily. "You'll scare her." He ran after Rosie, but by the time he got the ball back, it was nearly the end of break.

"That was handball," said Smithy. "It's a penalty!"

That's Smithy for you. He's brilliant at football, but sometimes he's a real pain. He aimed his shot for the corner of the goal, but I saved it, no trouble. I was so mad at Smithy that I whacked the ball down the pitch as hard as I could.

That's when I saw Mrs Bird. What was she doing there? She didn't see the ball flying towards her until it was too late. It hit her right between the eyes.

Everyone stopped. Mrs Bird stood there with her mouth open. There was

a round muddy mark on her fore-
head. Then she started to scream. She
screamed and screamed. Mrs Kingsley
came running out of the school.

"A football!" gasped Mrs Bird. "It
came out of nowhere. These children
. . . they're mad. Completely mad."

"But Mrs Kingsley . . ." I began.

"Don't say a word, Felicity Parker,"
she snapped. "This class has reduced
three teachers to gibbering wrecks.

It cannot go on. I have just finished interviewing Mrs MacKay's replacement. I think you'll find that she is a bit tougher than . . ."

Mrs Bird coughed.

"Yes, well," Mrs Kingsley continued, "let's just say I think Miss Brown is the right woman for the job." I didn't like the sound of Miss Brown. But Mrs Kingsley hadn't finished.

"If it's football you want," she said grimly, "then I'll give you football. Oh yes! I'll give you football all right."

Mrs Kingsley smiled. She seemed to be very pleased with herself. But everyone knew that Mrs Kingsley *hated* football. She obviously had some dark secret. But we were going to have to wait until Monday to find out what it was.

Chapter Three
The Church Street Gang

When I got to the rec. on Saturday morning the Church Street gang were there. They were playing on *our* pitch. I pretended I hadn't seen them, and I sat down on the swings to wait for the others.

The Church Street gang were bad news. They all went to Church Street

Primary – the only other school in town. Unlike us, Church Street Primary had a football team. They were famous for never losing a match in the Inter-Schools League. They were also famous for being mean, nasty, and horrible – and that wasn't just the way they looked. They played football that way too. We tried to keep out of their way if we possibly could.

"Hey!" Smithy came charging through the gates. Leroy, Jack, Danny, and Sanjay were right behind him. He marched onto the pitch – straight up to Buster. All the kids in the Church Street football team were mean, but Buster was worse than any of them. Sometimes Smithy has no sense at all.

"This is *our* pitch," Smithy said.

"Since when?"

"We always play here."

"Yeah?" Buster looked around. "Tough luck. It's a dump, isn't it? But our park's closed today. Tell you what – we'll give you a game."

"There's six of you," said Smithy, "and there's only five of us."

"Six," I said. "There's six of us, too. You forgot about me, Smithy." He hadn't forgotten about me, of course. He just thought the Church Street gang would laugh at him for playing with a girl. He was right.

"Who's captain?" said Buster. "You? Or your girlfriend?" The rest of the Church Street gang fell about laughing at this brilliant joke.

"I'm not his girlfriend," I said. "I'm the goalkeeper. And I'll stop your pathetic shots, no trouble."

"Fine," said Buster. He chucked the ball at me – hard. "You kick off. First to ten, OK? Should take at least five minutes."

Chapter Four
Foul!

Danny kicked off. He tapped the ball to Smithy. Buster charged. I could see what he was going to do. You see everything when you're in goal. Buster didn't even *try* to get the ball. He smashed into Smithy with his shoulder and Smithy went flying. I heard him yell as he landed. I saw his leg twist.

"Foul!" screamed Leroy. Not much point doing *that*. There was no referee, and there was no way Church Street were going to stop. The ball rocketed around the pitch.

"Square ball, Rixy!"

"Down the line, Spud!"

"Cross it, Ginger!"

Smithy was still trying to get to his

feet. Buster hurled himself through the air. I dived, but it was no use. No-one could have stopped it.

"One—nil," said Buster. "Who's pathetic now?"

"You are," I said. "You fouled him. You fouled Smithy. That goal doesn't count."

Buster laughed. "Did you hear a whistle blow? Your boyfriend can't take a tackle, that's his trouble."

Smithy stood up. As soon as he tried to walk, his ankle gave way.

"I . . . I think it might be broken," he said. His face had gone a funny shade of green, and there were tears in his eyes.

"You're chicken, that's all," sneered Buster. "It's not surprising you haven't got a school team. Your captain's a crybaby, and you let a girl go in goal. You're useless."

The Church Street gang jumped on their bikes and screamed off out of the gates.

Chapter Five

Miss Brown

When we arrived in our classroom on
Monday morning, there was no sign
of the new teacher. Smithy's ankle
wasn't broken, but it had swollen up
like a pumpkin. Smithy
had crutches, so he
was practising being
Long John Silver.
Ronaldo was sup-
posed to be his
parrot, but
Ronaldo wouldn't
stay on Smithy's
shoulder. That's
why Leroy was
on a guinea-pig
hunt under the
tables.

"Look what I've got," said Danny. He pulled a mini-football out of his bag. He chucked it in the air and headed it to me. I headed it on to Jack. He sent it looping across the classroom towards Sanjay.

That's when the door opened, and Miss Brown walked in. She saw the ball in mid-air, and she dropped her briefcase on the floor. She reached out a foot, flipped the ball up, and caught it in one hand. Then she put it down on her desk as if that was the sort of thing she did every day of the week.

"Sit down, Class Five," Miss Brown said.

We were too astonished to do anything else. Mrs Kingsley followed Miss Brown into the room.

"I see you've made an impression already, Miss Brown," said Mrs Kingsley. "Now then Class Five, you'll be thrilled to know that Miss Brown is a *veteran* football player." Miss Brown didn't look too happy at being called a veteran. She was young and she looked incredibly fit. But Mrs Kingsley carried on anyway.

"Miss Brown played for England Women, you know. 1991, wasn't it, Miss Brown?" Miss Brown smiled. She had blue eyes and there were little crinkles around them.

"Well," continued Mrs Kingsley, "I'll leave Miss Brown to tell you the rest of the good news. Have fun, Class

Five." She walked past me on her way out. Mrs Kingsley was *singing* under her breath. I pinched myself to make sure I wasn't dreaming.

Miss Brown looked around the classroom. No-one moved a muscle. We could hear the kids in the other classes chattering. I put my hand up.

"Did you *really* play for England?" I asked.

"Ah," she said. "You must be Felicity Parker. I've heard a great deal about *you*. I hear there has been a problem about football."

"It wasn't our fault," I said. I was going to tell her all about it, but Miss Brown was full of surprises.

"Quite so. Just what I told Mrs Kingsley. I told her you needed a challenge. A match with another school would be just the ticket."

Everyone cheered. It was exactly what we'd always wanted. A school team at last.

"Silence!" Suddenly, the blue eyes didn't look so kind any more. Then something moved under one of the tables.

"Come out of there at once!" There was no doubt now – Miss Brown's eyes were flashing with anger. Leroy stood up sheepishly. He was holding Ronaldo in one hand.

"Sorry," he said. "It's Ronaldo. He escaped."

"I don't care if it's Michael Owen," said Miss Brown. "Put that animal back in its cage this instant. Let's get things straight. There will be training before school and after school. Also on Saturday mornings. No team coached by me has ever lost a match, and I'm not about to start losing now. I'm told the opposition are tough. Mrs Kingsley says they have *never* been beaten."

I had this sinking feeling. She could only be talking about one team. I was right.

"Three weeks today," said Miss Brown, "we will play a friendly match against Church Street Primary School. And *we* will win."

Chapter Six

Of Course She's Going in Goal

"A *friendly*! Against Church Street?"
said Leroy at break. "What a joke!
Most probably none of us will
survive. In fact, that's probably what
Mrs Kingsley's hoping for. Then she'll
have a nice quiet school."

"But we've got Miss Brown," I said.
"You heard her. She's never lost a match."

"She says!"

"Yeah," said Danny, "and I bet none of her other teams ever played Church Street."

"AND Smithy's injured," said Jack. "We won't even have a decent team."

All of them were grumbling. I couldn't believe it. Then Smithy arrived, hopping across the playground on his crutches.

"It's OK," Smithy said. "The doctor says I can start playing again in about a week. By that time you should all be nearly as good as me. Great, isn't it? I can't wait to see the look on Buster's face when we beat them."

It's always the same. They won't listen to *me*. But *Smithy* – that's different. Suddenly they were all talking about who would be in the team, and what position they'd play. I knew

they'd only remember me when they
needed a goalie. Well, I was going to
show them. Now we had a proper
team and a proper coach, I just *knew*
my chance was going to come.

The training began the next morning. We all got to school half an hour
early. Mrs Kingsley and Miss Brown
were waiting for us.

"I never thought I'd see the day," said
our headteacher. "Class Five early for
school. Jolly well done, Miss Brown."

I never thought *I'd* see the day when Mrs Kingsley turned up at school in a pink tracksuit and trainers. And then there was Miss Brown. She was scary in the classroom, but she was *terrifying* on the football pitch. She was wearing her England kit and bouncing a ball on her foot while she chatted to Mrs Kingsley. She never dropped it *once*.

I kept thinking about what I had
to say to Miss Brown. I needed to say
it before it was too late. I felt sick. But
I had to do it.

"Miss Brown?"

"Yes, Felicity?"

"I don't have to go in goal, do I?"

The others groaned.

"Of course she's going in goal,"
said Smithy, swinging between his
crutches. "She's the only one who's
any good."

OK, so I'm good in goal. As it
happens, I'm good at just about
everything. But none of them understand. I want to dazzle people with
my ball skills, not hop up and down
on the goal line, waiting for something to happen.

"Alexander, when I want your
advice, I'll ask for it." Miss Brown was
annoyed. Smithy went red. He

hopped away to sit on a bench. Did I mention that Smithy's real name is Alexander? *He* thinks Alexander is worse than Felicity. That shows how much *he* knows about anything.

"But Miss Brown — I will get a chance, won't I?" I said.

"Oh yes, Felicity," Miss Brown replied. There was an expression on her face I didn't like the look of. There was a steely glint in her eyes. "Things have been sloppy around here," she went on. "Very sloppy. It's a terrible thing to see all this talent going to waste. So, you're all going to work like you've never worked before. Let's get started."

She wasn't joking. By the end of

the day, I was so stiff I could hardly walk. And we didn't play one single game of football! Just practise, practise, practise.

"I don't think I like football any more," said Danny when the after-school training session was finally over. We were hobbling along Hillside Road. Leroy had borrowed one of Smithy's crutches.

"Another day of this," he said, limping along the pavement, "and I'll need a wheelchair."

I told him not to be so pathetic. Some people just don't have the will to win. Then we saw them. The Church Street gang. There was no way we could escape.

"Mr Potter says we've got to play against you," Buster sneered. "We told him it wasn't worth it. We told him you were rubbish. We even told him you had a girl in goal. But he said we had to play you anyway."

"You wait," I said. "It'll be different when there's a referee. It'll be different when you can't just *kick* people."

Buster grinned at me. It was a horrible sight. "Football's a tough game, *Felicity*," he said.

I don't know how he'd found out my name, but I wished he hadn't. "Sometimes people get hurt.

Referees don't make any difference.
That's just the way it is."

I shivered. I couldn't help myself.
I knew he was just a pathetic creep.
But the trouble was, he was scary too.
I had the feeling that even *with* a
referee, playing against Church Street
might be more like a battle than a
football match.

Chapter Seven
Brazil

"Today," said Miss Brown, "I'm going to explain to you how we will beat Church Street."

We were all too exhausted to cheer. And I don't think a single one of us thought we had the tiniest chance of beating Church Street. Well, maybe Smithy did, but *he'd* just spent a restful week sitting on a bench watching *us* going through torture. We'd run and jogged and sprinted and jumped. We'd learnt to control the ball with every single part of our bodies (except our hands, of course). And we hadn't played *one* proper game of football.

Miss Brown pulled down the blinds and switched on the TV. "Just watch," she said. "Oh, and count the passes.

Then we can tell Mrs Kingsley we're doing maths, if she asks."

It was Brazil on the video. There were thirty-two passes before their striker, Pelé, headed the ball past the keeper. It was incredible.

"But we can't do that," I said, when it finished.

"Oh yes, you can!" said Miss Brown. "Don't you see? It's so simple. You control the ball quickly, you pass it perfectly, and you move." Her eyes

41

were shining. "Football like that is beautiful to watch. It's the best football in the world. And *that* is how *you* are going to play."

That afternoon we played our first practice match. I was in goal. OK, I know I said I didn't want to, but I didn't dare keep complaining. Our team had all the best players. Jack and Leroy in defence, Sanjay and Danny in attack, and Brian in midfield. But we weren't a bit like Brazil. When we had finished, I could see that Miss Brown was disappointed. I felt sorry for her.

"It'll be all right," I said. "The doctor says Smithy can play tomorrow. We'll be much better when Smithy's playing."

"And how about you, Felicity?" Miss Brown asked suddenly. "Your ball control is pretty good. I've been watching you. Are you ready to have a go in midfield?" My voice stopped working. I tried to speak, but all I could do was nod and squeak.

"Excellent," Miss Brown said. "Brian, you go in goal."

I looked over at Smithy, sitting on his bench. I waved to him. I thought he'd be pleased, but he looked the other way.

Sanjay kicked off, then Jack passed the ball back to me. I controlled it quickly. I could see Sanjay running and I hit my pass *instantly*. Martin's tackle was too late. I skipped away from him. I saw Sanjay kill the ball, and I yelled to him. I pointed to the empty space where I wanted him to pass. It was perfect. I touched the ball forward and I heard Leroy shout. He had raced down the wing. I knew what to do. I'd seen the Brazilians do it. I kicked the ball with the *outside* of my foot. It curled round a defender and landed right in front of Leroy.

He didn't hesitate. He chipped it first time, back across the penalty area. Sanjay was there. He volleyed it into the roof of the net.

Miss Brown blew the whistle. She had a huge smile on her face.

"That was wonderful!" she said.

"Now you can see what I mean. If you play like that, you can beat absolutely anyone! Felicity, you are a natural!"

I felt as if I was going to burst with pride. When the game finished, I ran over to Smithy.

"Did you see that, Smithy?" I asked him. "Excellent, or what?"

"So who's going to go in goal then?" was all he said. "You know you're the only decent goalie we've got."

"Who cares?" I told him. "Didn't you *see*, Smithy? We were *fantastic*! Just like Brazil. And when we've got you playing too . . . We won't even need a goalie. Church Street won't even touch the ball."

"Oh yeah?" said Smithy. And he gave me a really funny look as he walked off across the playground.

Chapter Eight
A Crazy Idea

OK, I should have realized. Smithy saw us playing brilliantly, and he couldn't see how *he* was going to get in the team. And whose fault was that? Mine, of course. That's what Smithy thought. That's why he wouldn't talk to me on the way home. Or next morning either, when he came to training for the first time.

When we'd finished the warm-ups Smithy looked as if he'd been for a ten-mile run. He was exhausted. Of course, it wasn't *his* fault that he wasn't fit. But that's when I realized how fit the rest of us were. Miss Brown's plan was working.

"Right, Alexander," Miss Brown said. "Let's see how you slot in to the team. You can play up front alongside Jack. Danny – you go on the other team."

"But . . ." Danny was really fed up. He'd been great the day before. It didn't seem fair. There wasn't time to worry about it though. Smithy kicked off and Jack passed the ball to me.

"Yours, Smithy!" I yelled, and I sent a curving Brazilian pass flying into the space in front of him. He started to run, but then he just gave up. He turned round and shouted at me.

"I can't get *that*! Pass it properly."

I couldn't believe my ears. It had been a *perfect* pass! Or it would have been if Smithy had tried. A few minutes later I had the ball again. I heard Smithy shouting for it. Right, I thought, see what you can do with *this* – and I passed it straight to his feet. He couldn't grumble about that.

He took the ball, and he started to dribble. He didn't bother to look and see if there was anyone to pass to. He beat one player, and then there were two more in front of him. He should have passed, but he just kept on going – and of course, he lost the ball.

The defender passed it to Danny – a terrific pass, right down the pitch. Danny steadied himself and hit the shot. Brian in goal was far too slow. He dived for the ball and it slid through his hands. Miss Brown blew the whistle.

"Fine," she said, "I've seen enough. Brian, I somehow don't think you're cut out to be a goalie." Brian grinned and shook his head. "And Alexander, I know you've been injured, but I'm surprised you've not understood our tactics. I think Danny's better in that position. Which leaves us with a problem . . ."

For a few seconds none of us knew what Miss Brown was talking about. Then we realized. We didn't have a goalie. And Miss Brown was looking at Smithy. I saw the look on Smithy's face, and I couldn't stop myself laughing. I tried to turn it into a cough, but Smithy had seen. And some of the others grinned too. It was a crazy idea – Smithy in goal.

"Well, Alexander?" said Miss Brown. "Will you give it a try?"

He didn't really have any choice.

"I knew it," he muttered, as he pulled on the gloves. "I just knew it."

Chapter Nine
A Well-Oiled Machine

Smithy went on the other team, and Danny came back on our side to play up front. Everything was just the way it had been the day before. We passed and we ran. The other team couldn't get near us. It was the most exciting thing ever. Then suddenly I had the ball at my feet, and only

Smithy to beat. I looked into his eyes
– and I wished I hadn't.

Smithy was angry. He wasn't angry
with *himself* for being so selfish when he
had the chance to impress Miss Brown.
Not Smithy. And he wasn't angry with
Buster either, for hurting his leg and
making him miss all that training. He
was angry with *me*! And of course, that
made *me* mad too.

I hit a *wicked* shot. It curved
and then it dipped. But
Smithy simply *flew* across
the goal. It must have
been the anger that
made him fly.

He stood up with the ball in his hands. It was the most amazing save I had ever seen.

"Incredible!" gasped Miss Brown.

"But I didn't mean . . . it was an accident," Smithy stammered.

"Some accident," said Miss Brown. "What a relief. I was starting to think we'd never find a goalie. Every great team needs a solid goalkeeper – and now we've found one. Well done, Alexander. The position is yours!"

Miss Brown changed everything round then. She put Smithy in goal on our team.

"Wonderful," she said. "From now on, you will play together all the time. Alexander in goal. Leroy and Jack in defence, Sanjay and Danny up front, and Felicity in midfield. I want you to be like a well-oiled machine. I want you to be able to pass to each other with your eyes shut. And, just to keep you on your toes, I'll go on the other side."

We played practice matches every day. And now we *really* had something to think about. Miss Brown was everywhere! Every time someone passed to me, Miss Brown was waiting to snatch it away. I didn't see how I'd *ever* get quick enough to beat her. But then, slowly, as the days went by, we all began to improve. Even with Miss Brown waiting to pounce, I could control the ball and make a perfect pass.

There was just one person who didn't improve. Between the goalposts, Smithy sulked and sulked.

After training on Friday night, with only three days to go before the big match, Miss Brown said, "I'm wondering, Alexander, if we wouldn't be better off with Brian in goal after all."

"I don't care," muttered Smithy. "Do what you like." He headed for the door.

Miss Brown was angry. "Come here, Alexander," she began.

"Please," I said to Miss Brown, "don't be cross. He doesn't mean it. I'll go after him. Smithy *will* go in goal. I know he will."

Chapter Ten

He Couldn't Stop a Balloon

I caught up with Smithy on the corner of Wood Street.

"Smithy! Wait!"

He tried to keep on walking, so I stood in front of him.

"Get out of my way, *Felicity*."

"You're just trying to make me mad," I said. "Well it won't work.

We're a team, Smithy. Someone's got to go in goal."

"It doesn't have to be me though, does it? You could go and tell Miss Brown *you'll* go in goal. Then I wouldn't have to. I could go in midfield. This is all your fault."

"My fault!" I said. "*My* fault? How can it be my fault? I *knew* that's what you were thinking. The only time you managed to make a decent save was when you were mad at me. And even if I did go in goal, what makes you think you'd get in the team? Don't you care about the rest of us? You'd be a brilliant keeper if you tried. Far better than me."

"Him? In goal? Don't make me laugh. He couldn't stop a balloon."

It was Buster. We'd been so busy arguing that we hadn't seen them coming – the Church Street gang.

We were trapped.

Smithy seemed to grow about ten centimetres.

"You'll see," he said. "I can save anything your flabby legs can hit at me, that's for sure."

"You what?"

"I said . . ." began Smithy.

"Leave it," I told him. "They'll find out soon enough." I was staring at Smithy. A few seconds before he had been moaning about being in goal, and now he was telling Buster how brilliant he was going to be.

Sometimes I think I'll *never* understand him.

"That's it," sneered Buster. "Do what your girlfriend tells you."

"I'm *not* his girlfriend," I said.

"And you're not the goalie now either. What happened? Did they chuck you out of the team? At least they've got *some* sense."

He pushed me against the wall. I could smell his disgusting breath. "As it happens," I said, "I'm playing in midfield." He started to laugh.

"We'll run rings round you," I said, and I shoved him, *hard*. He was so surprised that he nearly fell over. Rixy caught him.

"Run, Smithy," I yelled. And we did. We stopped outside his gate, gasping for air.

"At least we know we're faster than them," I said.

Smithy grinned.

"Yeah," he said. "And I suppose I've been a bit stupid. Look, Fizz, did you mean it? You know . . . when you said I could be good in goal."

"I wouldn't have said it if I didn't mean it," I told him.

Smithy still looked worried. "But Miss Brown might not let me play now," he said.

"Of course she will," I told him. "You're the best goalie we've got. Miss Brown knows that — and she wants to win."

I was trying to sound confident, but Miss Brown *had* looked mad, and inside I was wishing that I hadn't shoved Buster. At least not *quite* so hard. It was one thing playing against our 'B' team and Miss Brown. *She* didn't foul. But it wasn't going to be much fun playing against Church Street. And on Monday afternoon, we were going to have to do it.

Chapter Eleven
They'll Pulverize Us

I couldn't sleep on Sunday night.
Every time I started to doze off, I had
a nightmare where Buster was
coming at me like a monster in a
horror movie. And then I'd wake up
and realize that it was true. It was
actually going to happen.

I was right about Miss Brown. She tried to look strict and teachery when she told Smithy he could play but anyone could see she was pleased. Smithy was so excited that he didn't even seem to notice how nervous the rest of us were. Then, at half past three, we all looked out of the window to watch Church Street arrive.

"They've got matching tracksuits," gasped Leroy as Buster and his mates climbed out of the minibus.

"*And* they've got their names on the back," Sanjay groaned.

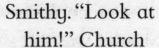

"And look!" said Smithy. "Look at him!" Church Street's teacher climbed out of the bus – Mr Potter. He was a big, red-faced man with a moustache. He was wearing a track-suit too – with *his* name on the back. Mrs Kingsley and Miss Brown were there to meet him and they held out their hands. Mr Potter ignored them. He waved his arms about a lot. He seemed to be complaining about something.

"I think I'm ill," said Leroy. "I

thought this morning maybe I was getting the flu. Now I know it. I'm off." But before he could move, Miss Brown burst in through the classroom door. I thought she was going to explode.

"Unbelievable!" she fumed. "The nerve of some people! That man! Complaining about the changing facilities! In a primary school." She stopped. "What are you staring at?" she demanded. Then she looked more closely. We were all shivering. Even Smithy had gone pale now.

"What on earth is the matter with you lot?" she demanded.

"Miss Brown," said Leroy, "they'll foul us. You don't know what they're like."

"Oh, but I do," Miss Brown replied, "I took the precaution of watching Church Street play. I watched them beat Snipperton Primary School eleven–nil. It wasn't a pretty sight."

"Exactly," said Smithy. "They'll pulverize us."

"Listen to me," snapped Miss Brown. "I've trained you to play beautiful, brilliant football. Total football. As far as I can see, this lot are a nothing but a bunch of bullies. They think they can scare us. Well, they don't scare me – and they shouldn't scare you either. Because you are a million times better than they will ever be."

Miss Brown glared at us, daring us to argue. I was just glad that *she* wasn't playing against us.

"Off you go," she said. "Show them how the game should be played."

We clattered out of the school and across the playground in our brand new kit with the green and orange

stripes. The crowd cheered like mad.
All our mums and dads were there.
Even Mrs MacKay was there, with
her tiny new baby in her arms.

Then the whistle blew, and I heard Miss Brown saying, "Go on, Felicity. The ref wants you. It's time to toss up."

"Me?" I said. "You mean . . ?"

"That's right," said Miss Brown. "You're the captain."

I felt numb. I felt like I was in a dream. I walked towards the centre circle – and then I saw the ref. It was Mr Potter – the teacher from Church Street.

Chapter Twelve

They've Even Got the Ref on Their Side

"Where's the captain?" demanded Mr Potter. "Really! This is ridiculous."

"*I'm* the captain," I told him.

He stared at me. "You?" he said. "Unbelievable! Do you know how to toss up? You choose heads or tails . . ."

"Heads," I said. I could see why Miss Brown had been so angry.

Buster and his mates obviously thought Mr Potter was fantastically funny. They were doubled up, laughing. We've just *got* to beat them, I thought, as I watched the coin spinning in the air.

"Tails," said Mr Potter. "Church Street to kick off."

I ran back to where the rest of the team were warming up in front of our goal. I clapped my hands. "This is it," I said. "They think they're so brilliant. But we can run rings round them. You know we can. Tell them, Smithy." But Smithy looked *green*.

"They've even got the ref on their side," he said. "We'll all be in *hospital* by six o'clock."

There wasn't time to argue. Mr Potter was peeping his whistle impatiently. Danny and Sanjay trudged up the field to take up their positions and I jogged into the centre of our half. I *knew* we could win if we played the way Miss Brown had shown us, but the others seemed to have given up already. Then Buster kicked off. He tapped the ball to Rixy and he ran straight at me.

It was just like my nightmares. I was sweating. I remembered what he'd done to Smithy. Then I thought, *he can't — there's a ref.* Big mistake!

I tried to get out of the way, but as Buster raced past me he hooked his boot around my ankle, and suddenly I was flying through the air. I rolled over a couple of times and bounced to my feet.

"Ref!" I yelled. "Foul!"

"He didn't touch you," said Mr Potter as he ran past. "You'll have to do better than that, young lady." Out on the wing, Ginger had the ball. Leroy was marking him tightly.

"You OK?" asked Sanjay.

"You bet," I said. Then I saw the look on Sanjay's face. He wasn't scared any more. He was as angry as I was. And I saw Danny racing back to help out. Now we *really* had a chance.

"Come on!" I yelled. "We can do it!"

But right at that moment, Ginger crossed the ball and Buster's header blasted towards our goal.

Chapter Thirteen
Pure Genius

My eyes zoomed in on Smithy's face.
He was staring into space, and he
hadn't moved.

'SMITHY!!!" I screamed. I saw his
eyes snap into focus, and everything
seemed to happen at once. Buster's
head connected with the ball. Smithy
launched himself. His outstretched

fingers brushed against the ball as it
flew by, forcing it up and against the
crossbar. It bounced down fiercely, hit
the back of Smithy's head – and
rolled across the line. Mr Potter
peeped his whistle. "One–nil, Church
Street," he said, and he wrote care-
fully in his small black notebook.

I ran back and grabbed the ball out of the net. "Not your fault," I told Smithy. "We should have known they'd try that. Exactly what they did at the rec. Only you nearly saved that one. I wouldn't have got near it."

Smithy shook his head. "But I didn't save it, did I? And now we're one–nil down."

"You wait," I said. "Now we're going to really show them. Total football. Relax, Smithy. You probably won't have to make another save."

I ran back to the centre and placed the ball. I looked at Buster and his mates. They thought it was all over. Buster pointed at me and said something to Rixy, then they both hooted with laughter. I felt icy cool.

"This is it," I said to Danny. "Let's show them what we can do. Let's make them look even more stupid than they really are."

Danny kicked off, and Sanjay played the ball back to me. Buster came charging towards me, but this time I was ready. I stroked the ball to Danny with my left foot, and sprinted off in the opposite direction. Buster tried to get the ball with one foot, and he tried to foul me with the other one. He collapsed in a heap on the ground.

Danny had controlled the ball perfectly, and as I ran towards the

penalty area I saw him hit a pass to
Sanjay. Sanjay knew just where I was.
He flicked the ball on towards me
before the defender had even realized
what was happening. Buster was still
climbing to his feet as I volleyed the
ball past the goalkeeper. The scores
were level, and the Church Street
players were stunned. Miss Brown's
voice came from the touchline.

"Genius!" she yelled. "Pure genius!
Keep it up, Hillside."

"Pure luck, more like," muttered
Mr Potter, as he wrote the goal into
his notebook.

For the rest of the first half, we
were brilliant. There's no other word
for it. OK, maybe not as good as
Brazil, but Church Street hardly
touched the ball. The only trouble
was, we just couldn't score. We hit the
bar twice, and the post once, and

their goalie made four or five brilliant saves.

"Just keep it up," said Miss Brown, when half time arrived. "Don't panic. And even if you don't score the winner, I'm proud of you all. I could watch football like that all day long."

"And I must say," put in Mrs Kingsley, "that I quite agree. I never knew football could be so . . . so . . ."

"Exciting?" I said.

"Thrilling?" asked Miss Brown with a smile.

"*Beautiful*," sighed Mrs Kingsley.

"And it will be even more beautiful," I said, "if we can actually beat them."

Miss Brown looked at Mrs Kingsley. They both looked over to where Mr Potter was shouting at the Church Street team. They both smiled. "Too right," they said together.

Chapter Fourteen
Nice One, Smithy

It was our kick-off. I watched the faces of the Church Street team as they walked back onto the pitch. They didn't look so confident any more. Even Buster couldn't think of anything clever to shout at us as Danny nudged the ball to Sanjay.

We carried on just the way we'd

finished the first half, but now it was even more difficult to score. Church Street had finally realized that they weren't going to be able to *scare* us into playing badly, and now *they* started trying to play football themselves – instead of just trying to foul. The minutes ticked away, and still we couldn't score. I knew we had to do something special – something they weren't expecting. I looked at Smithy. He hadn't had to make a single save. He was jogging backwards and forwards. He looked ready for action. And Miss Brown *did* say she wanted to win. The next time the ball went out for a throw-in I ran back to Smithy. I told him my idea.

"But I can't," he said. "How can I? We haven't practised doing that. Miss Brown will go crazy."

"Do you want to win or not?" I

asked him. Then he grinned. He looked at the exhausted Church Street players.

"You're on," he said. "You say when, and I'll do it."

He didn't have to wait long. I had the ball, just inside the centre circle. Rixy was chasing after me, and suddenly he stopped and bent double. He had a stitch. I looked over to the touchline.

"One minute!" called Miss Brown.

"Come on, Hillside!" shouted Mrs Kingsley.

"NOW, SMITHY!!!" I yelled, and I passed the ball out to Sanjay on the wing. Smithy came screaming out of his goal. He was like a guided missile. Sanjay flicked the ball inside to me. I controlled it. Smithy was inside the Church Street half now, and heading for goal. Buster had seen the danger and was going after him, so now Jack

was free on the left wing. I curved a
perfect pass to him. He touched the
ball forward and crossed it beautifully
towards Smithy's head.

Smithy and Buster
reached the ball at
almost the same
moment. Smithy
ducked, and the
ball flew past
him. Buster
yelled. He
thought
he'd done it.
He thought
the danger
had gone.
I watched the ball falling towards me,
just the way we'd planned, and then
I blasted it past the Church Street
keeper. Two–one to Hillside. Mr Potter
looked at his watch.

He looked at the Church Street players. The terrors of the Inter-Schools League had all collapsed on the ground. Even the terrible Buster had his head in his hands. There was no time left. Mr Potter blew his whistle for the end of the game. We had beaten Church Street Primary.
We would never be scared of *them* again.

The crowd went wild. The little
kids from Year One invaded the pitch.
All the mums and dads invaded the
pitch. Mrs MacKay and her little *baby*
invaded the pitch. Miss Brown and
Mrs Kingsley were right behind them.

"Wonderful, Fizz!" yelled Mrs
Kingsley. "Magnificent, Smithy!"

I couldn't believe my ears. Mrs Kingsley had called me Fizz!

"Terrific game, *everyone*," Miss Brown said. She marched up to Mr Potter. "Tremendous news, Mr Potter," she announced in her loudest voice.

Everyone stopped and listened. Miss Brown had a piece of paper in her hand. "These are the fixtures for the new season of the Inter-Schools

League. We've entered, you know. And guess who we're playing in two weeks' time. Church Street Primary!"

I thought Mr Potter would choke. He spluttered something, then he groaned as he looked at the fixture list.

Right, I thought — and I started looking for Buster. He saw me coming. He was surrounded by mums and dads and little kids. He was trapped. I grabbed his hand and shook it — hard. I looked into his eyes.

"Thanks for the game, Buster," I said. "I'm really looking forward to our next match."

Very slowly, Buster
turned red. I kept
holding his hand,
and he went redder
and redder. Tomato,
then beetroot. Finally, I
took pity on him. I let go of his hand
and he *raced* into the school. Even his
mates were laughing.

I turned round – and there was Smithy.

"Nice one, Fizz!" he said.

"Yeah," I replied, pumping his hand up and down. "Nice one, Smithy!"

THE END

SAMMY'S SUPER SEASON
Lindsay Camp

A cat who can play football?!

Harry's cat, Sammy, is no ordinary tabby – he's the star goalkeeper of the school football team. And it's not just Harry and his school-mates who are fans. Sammy's spectacular saves attract the attention of Mudchester United FC. Will Sammy be tempted to play in the Premiership, or would he rather be at home eating Katbix?

A very funny story about an amazing footballing cat – perfect for building reading confidence.

ISBN 0 552 546615

THE BIG TIME
Rob Childs

"This is where we belong — in the big time!"

Andrew and Chris Weston have both been invited to attend a special summer coaching course at one of the country's top football clubs. The brothers are determined to give it their best shot, hoping to impress United's scouts.

Another bonus is the chance to be ball boys at a World Cup qualifying match between England and Holland. But the big event turns out to be even more explosive than anyone could ever have guessed. . . !

ISBN 0 552 546828

THE BIG SEND-OFF
Rob Childs

'Off! Off! Off!'

Danebridge school football team – captained by goalie Chris Weston – have had a shaky season in the League, but a good Cup run. Now they face a crucial semi-final replay – a match they must win if they are to meet their arch-rivals, Shenby, in the Final.

Chris knows it's not going to be easy – especially as one of their top goalscorers is leaving at Easter and would miss the Final. But even he doesn't expect quite so much drama: everything from a nerve-jangling penalty shootout to a shock sending-off!

ISBN 0 552 546399